YOUNG  RE.

Rudyard Kipling

The Jungle Book

Retold by Richard B. A. Brown
Illustrated by Valentina Mai

This is the story of the Jungle Book. Perhaps you know the film? The cartoon with dancing bears and singing monkeys? It's a film for children, and people laugh when they watch it. It's funny.

But it's just a cartoon. It isn't real.

The real story of the Jungle Book isn't funny. You don't laugh when you read the real story.

If you don't like stories with blood and death, stop reading now. Find a different book, or watch a cartoon. Then you can laugh.

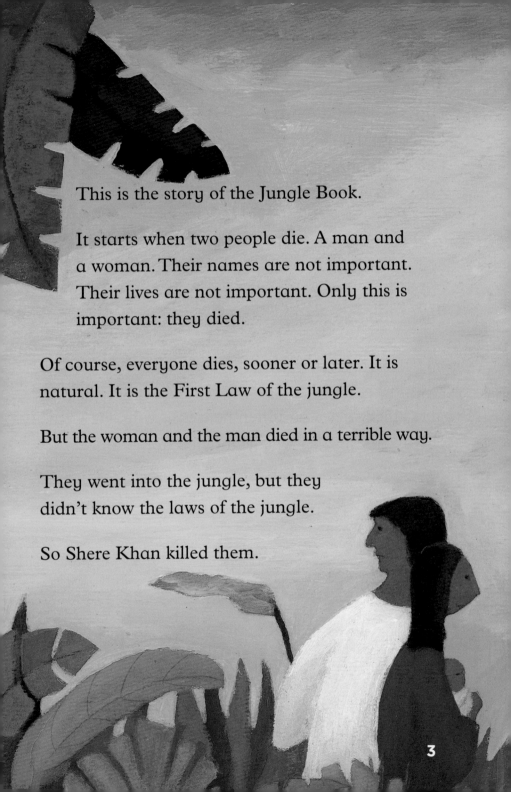

This is the story of the Jungle Book.

It starts when two people die. A man and
a woman. Their names are not important.
Their lives are not important. Only this is
important: they died.

Of course, everyone dies, sooner or later. It is
natural. It is the First Law of the jungle.

But the woman and the man died in a terrible way.

They went into the jungle, but they
didn't know the laws of the jungle.

So Shere Khan killed them.

One day in the jungle Shere Khan – the great
tiger – killed a man and a woman. He did this
because they were alone. He did this because
he was hungry. Hungry animals kill. This is
the Second Law of the jungle.

Animals do not understand fire. They call it
"The Orange Flower" and they are frightened
of it. Before they died, the man and the woman
used fire against Shere Khan.

They burned the great tiger. They burned his
paw – his foot – and Shere Khan was angry.
He killed them, and then he went away. He went
away because he was frightened of the fire.

We can call her Mother Wolf. Her
name was Raksha in the jungle.

She was in her home. She gave her
milk to her cubs, to her baby wolves.
Suddenly, she heard a noise, outside.
But she could not move.

A mother protects her cubs. This is the
Third Law of the jungle.

'Father Wolf,' she said to her husband,
'what is that noise?'
'It is Shere Khan,' he replied.
'No, I can hear another noise,' she said.
'Go outside, and see.'

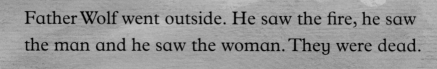

Father Wolf went outside. He saw the fire, he saw the man and he saw the woman. They were dead.

He did not see Shere Khan. The great tiger was not there.

And he saw a baby. The woman's baby. The baby was not dead.
'It is small,' he thought. 'It is like my wolf cubs, a man-cub.'

Raksha was sorry for the little man-cub.
He had no mother.

'I can call him Mowgli,' she said to her
husband. Mowgli is Little Frog in the
language of the jungle.

'Mowgli? It is a good name,' he replied.
'He is a little frog because he has no hair
on his body.'

Just then, there was a great
noise outside the wolves' home.

Shere Khan was back!

'Wolves!' he called. 'Wolves! Give me the man-cub.
Give me the man-cub now! I am very hungry!'

'This is my home,' said Raksha. 'In my home,
I decide. I am a Free Wolf!'

'Give me the man-cub. The man-cub is mine!'

'No, I say no!' replied Raksha. 'If you want the
man-cub, you must fight!'

One tiger cannot fight a group of wolves. Shere
Khan knew this. He could not win.

'Wolves!' he called. 'Wolves! I do not forget!
The man-cub is mine.'

Shere Khan walked slowly away. He was very angry.

'Wolves!' he called again from far. 'Wolves! When
I come back, I want the man-cub.'

Mowgli stayed with the wolf family.

The cubs grew, and Mowgli grew.
He learned the language of wolves.
He didn't learn the language of people.

He walked on two legs, and he walked
on four legs. He was a wolf!

Every wolf is part of a family, and every family is part of a pack.

A pack is a group of wolf families. A pack is stronger than a family. This is the Fourth Law of the jungle.

Akela was the strongest, bravest, most intelligent wolf. Akela was the leader of the pack.

Six months passed. It was time for the wolf meeting.

'Wolves of my pack,' Akela called. 'Wolves! It is time! Bring your cubs here. Bring them so the pack can see them.'

Every wolf family must bring its new cubs to the wolf meeting.

The cubs came out, one by one. The other wolves looked. They listened to the names of the cubs. They accepted the young wolves into the pack.

Then only one cub was left. Mowgli came into the centre of the pack.

'Someone must speak for the cub. Who can speak for this cub?' Akela asked.

A mother or father cannot speak for their cub. This is the Fifth Law of the jungle.

Nobody spoke. Mowgli the Little Frog was not a wolf.

'Who can speak for this cub?' Akela asked again.

'I can speak for this cub,' said Baloo the bear.
'I can speak for this man-cub who is a wolf and
who is not a wolf.'

'You know me,' Baloo continued. 'I am not a wolf
but I am a teacher of wolves. I teach the laws of
the jungle to your cubs. If you listen to me, I can
speak for this man-cub.'

'And I can speak for him,' said Bagheera the
black panther. 'I am a friend of the wolves. I can
speak for the Little Frog.'

Two friends spoke for Mowgli. In this way, he
became a member of the pack.

Mowgli stayed with the wolf pack. He studied with his brothers and sisters, the wolf cubs.

Baloo was a good teacher, and Mowgli learned the laws of the jungle and the languages of the animals.

He went with Bagheera, and he
learned to run and to hunt.

The years passed.

But Shere Khan did
not forget.

Years passed.

One day, Baloo spoke to Akela. Then he spoke to Bagheera, and to Raksha, and to Father Wolf. Finally he spoke to Mowgli.

'It is time,' he said. 'You know the laws of the jungle. Now you must learn the laws of people.'

Early one morning Bagheera took Mowgli to a village, and left him there.

Later, a woman found him. She took him into her house, and he lived with her family.

Mowgli stayed in the village. He did not like it, but he was patient. Be patient: this is the Sixth Law of the jungle.

Mowgli looked. He listened. He learned. He learned the Laws of People.

He learned to look after the cows. He learned to look after the fire.

The old men of the village talked about animals.
They didn't know anything. Mowgli knew.

They talked about ghosts, and spirits, and gods,
and about the jungle. They didn't know anything.
Mowgli knew.

'The jungle is wise,
but men are stupid,'
Mowgli thought.

Every evening Mowgli met his brother wolves in secret, near the village. Every evening they talked while the village slept. They told him about the jungle.

One evening, they told him Shere Khan was back. Mowgli decided to kill the great tiger.

The next morning, Mowgli took the cows out as usual.

He shouted 'Shere Khan! Shere Khan! Stupid Tiger! I am Mowgli, the Little Frog. I want

Shere Khan heard Mowgli. He was angry.
'The man-cub!' he thought. 'The man-cub is mine!'
He ran. He ran to fight Mowgli.

But Mowgli was not stupid. When the great tiger
came, Mowgli hit the cows with fire. The cows ran
forwards... the cows ran towards Shere Khan!

Shere Khan couldn't escape. There were too many
cows. They all ran forwards. The running cows
killed the great tiger.

Mowgli took the tiger skin back to the village.

'Did you kill the great tiger?' the people asked.
'Did you use strong magic to kill the great tiger?'

They were frightened. Mowgli was very strong.

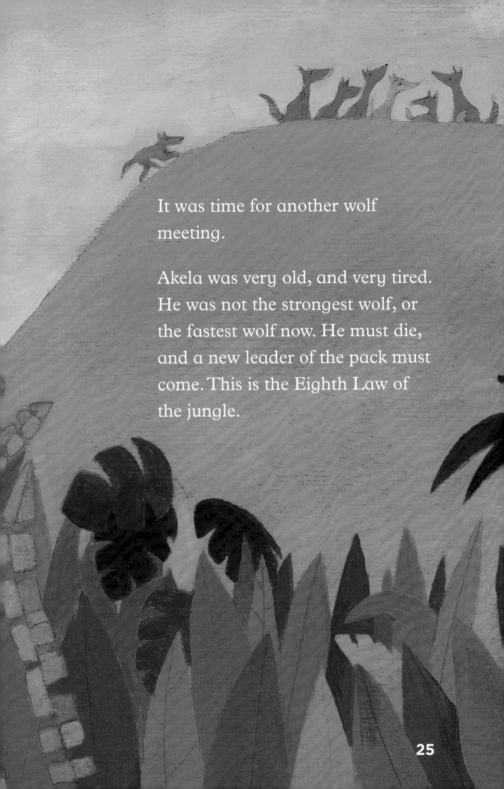

It was time for another wolf meeting.

Akela was very old, and very tired. He was not the strongest wolf, or the fastest wolf now. He must die, and a new leader of the pack must come. This is the Eighth Law of the jungle.

Suddenly, Mowgli was there. He had fire, the Orange Flower!

'Wolves!' he said, 'do not kill Akela. He is old but he is not bad.'

'It is the law of the jungle,' said a wolf. 'Akela must die.'

'Wolves!' replied the boy, 'I am Mowgli, the Little Frog. I am a wolf and I am not a wolf. I killed Shere Khan. I have fire, "The Orange Flower". I change the law!'

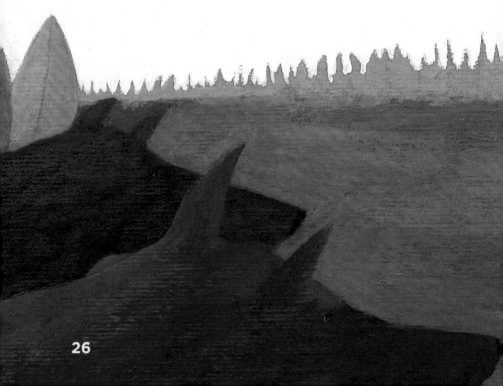

And that is the real story of the Jungle Book.

It started with blood, two dead people and a boy.
And it finished with blood, a dead tiger, a living
wolf and a boy who changed the laws of the
jungle.

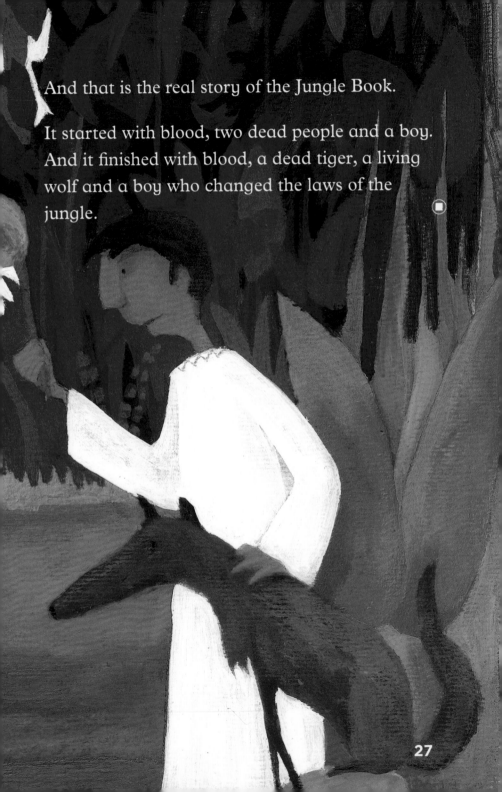

Activity Pages

1 Can you remember the story? Match each beginning to an end.

1 A man and a woman died but

2 Akela was the leader because

3 Baloo and Bagheera spoke for the baby so

4 Mowgli learned the language of animals and

5 Bagheera took him to a village and

6 Shere Khan coudn't escape because

7 Mowgli spoke to the wolves and

a the language of people.

b he joined the pack.

c he was the strongest.

d the cows ran very fast.

e they didn't kill the old wolf.

f a woman found him.

g their baby didn't.

2 Mowgli lived with the wolf family in their wolf home. Can you draw the wolf home?

3 Use the right form of these words to complete the sentences and tell the story.

change   ~~find~~   kill   learn   live   look   take   want

1 The wolves ___found___ a little baby in the jungle.

2 Shere Khan _____ to eat the little baby.

3 The wolves saved him, and he _____ with them.

4 He _____ the language of wolves.

5 Bagheera _____ him to a village.

6 He _____ after the cows.

7 He _____ the great tiger.

8 He _____ the laws of the jungle.

4 **Re-write the words in the correct order.**

1 the attacked the Shere man and woman. Khan

_____

2 baby. little Wolf Father the found

_____

3 of the learned jungle. Mowgli Laws the

_____

4 Akela pack. strongest in wolf was the the

_____

5 passed years but The Khan Shere forget. didn't

_____

6 cows. looked after the Mowgli

_____

7 Shere kill Khan Mowgli. didn't

_____

5 **Imagine this: you are in the story! Which character are you?**

6 Who said it? Match the words to the pictures.

1 I am a Free Wolf. _____

2 Who can speak for the man cub? _____

3 I am not a wolf, but I am a teacher of wolves.

_____

4 I do not forget. _____

5 Did you kill the great tiger? _____

6 He is old but he is not bad. _____

7 **Write and draw your answers.**

Who is the best character?   Who is the worst character?

Name:_____   Name:_____

Who is the funniest character?

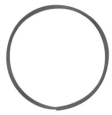

Name:_____

8 **What do you think? Draw your face.**

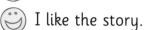 I like the story very much.

I like the story.

The story is OK.

 I don't like the story.